For John S. and Ari B. K.C

For Aldo. N.M

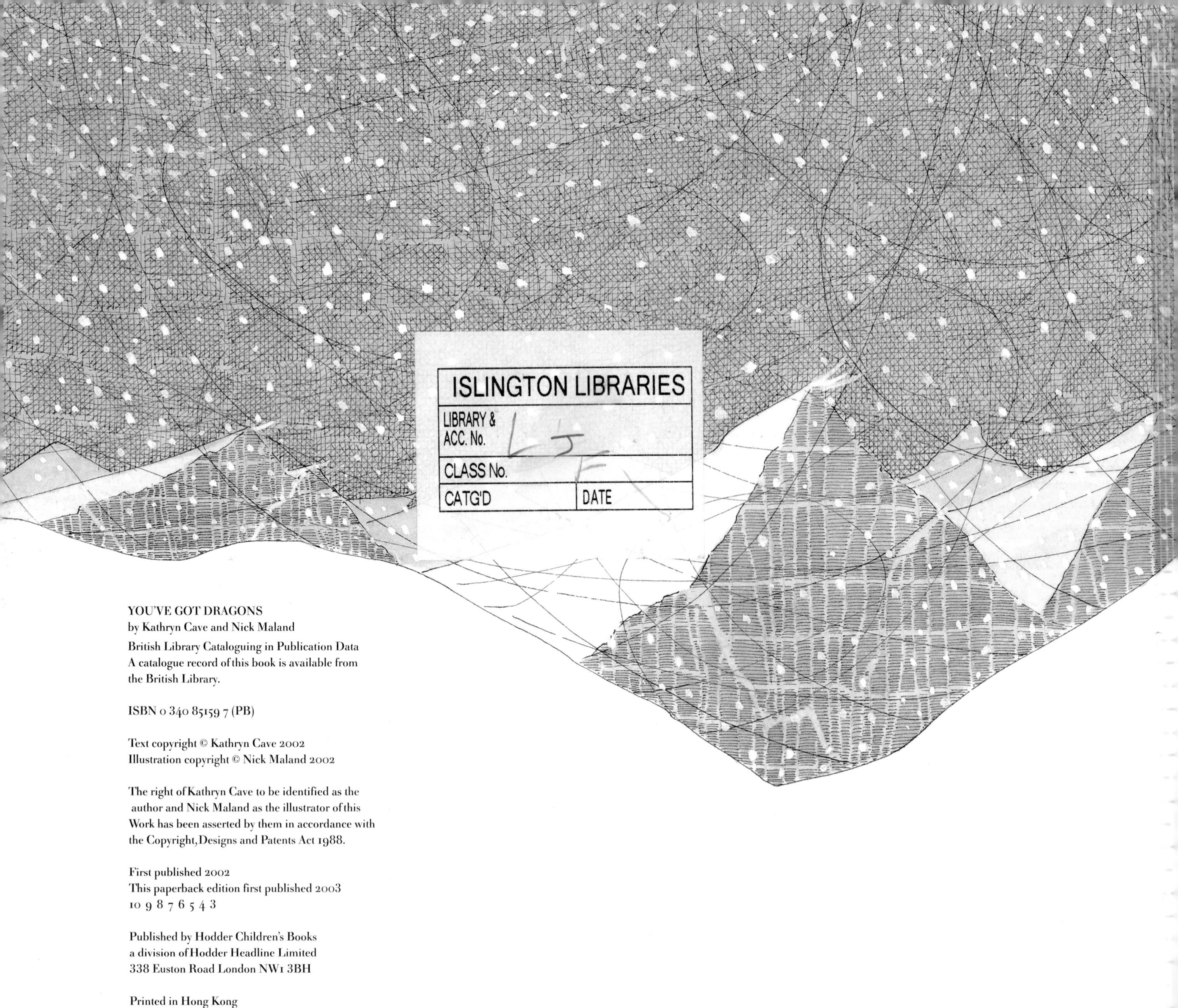

YOU'VE GOT DRAGONS
by Kathryn Cave and Nick Maland

British Library Cataloguing in Publication Data
A catalogue record of this book is available from the British Library.

ISBN 0 340 85159 7 (PB)

First published 2002
This paperback edition first published 2003
10 9 8 7 6 5 4 3

Published by Hodder Children's Books
a division of Hodder Headline Limited
338 Euston Road London NW1 3BH

Printed in Hong Kong

YOU'VE GOT DRAGONS

Written by Kathryn Cave

Illustrated by Nick Maland

A division of Hodder Headline Limited

Dragons come when you least expect them.
You turn round ...

. . . and they're **THERE.**

You think: *am I dreaming?*
And you pinch yourself, hard.

But you're not.

Your heart thuds and your knees wobble and your hands shake and your head whirls and you feel hot and cold and you can't seem to breathe and your tummy hurts and you can't believe it's really happening to you.

But it is. *It really is.*

Dragons don’t stay forever.
You think they will, but they won’t.

THIS is Montgomery, my maths-test dragon. He is dark red with orange claws and small green spots on his chest.

3. If you make your dragon laugh it will get smaller. Try telling it jokes.

This is Montgomery eating my maths teacher.

4. Remember to get plenty of hugs. Have one right now.

BEN'S TOP TIPS FOR WHEN YOU'VE GOT DRAGONS

1. Give your dragon your full attention at least once a day. Dragons get worse when ignored.

Greetings, honourable dragon.
Greetings, honourable Ben.

2. Really get to know your dragon. Give it a name. What sort of dragon is it? Look at it hard, then draw a picture.

Dear Dad,

Try under the stairs.

It's more comfy than under the bed. (I always wondered what you were doing there.)

Your loving son,

Ben.

PS: say 'Hi' to your dragons when they find you. They will.

Dear Ben,

I got dragons last month when we moved house. Now my tummy hurts each morning. Is this normal? I also have purple spots on my tongue. What do you suggest I do?

Yours anxiously,

Dave.

Dear Dave,

In answer to your letter:

1. *Yes*

2. *Stop chewing your felt-tips.* It makes your teeth purple too.

Your friend,

Ben.

Soon you are the world's greatest expert on having dragons.

By popular demand: **Ben's Problem Page**

Dear Ben,
I want to run away from my dragon. What kind of training should I do (I am six years old)? Also, do I need special shoes? If so, please tell me where I can get pink ones?
Yours sincerely,
Sophie.

Dear Sophie,
Special shoes and training won't help. Take it from me, dragons are too fast to run away from.
Yours,
Ben.

Dear Ben,
I have been trying to hide from my dragons for fifty-three years, eight months and four days. Can you recommend a foolproof hiding place?
Yours hopefully,
Dad.

When you've got dragons, you need lots of hugs.

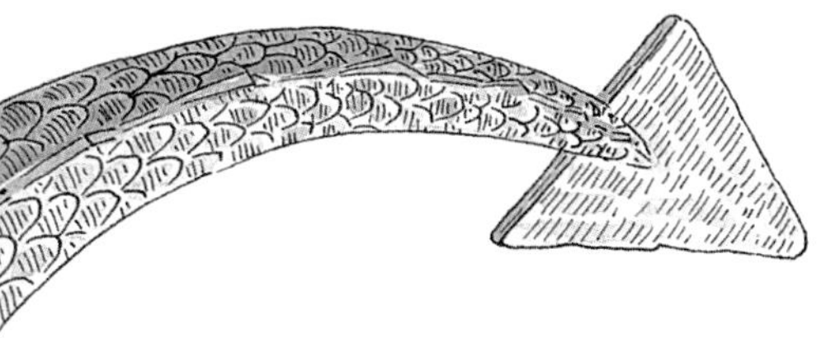

Sometimes you feel
you're burning up inside.
You want to shout at the
dragon: GO AWAY!
You'd like to stamp on it,
and kill it.

But it's bigger than you.

You'd need very big boots.

Sometimes you get cold and
shivery and you don't want to
be left on your own.

Dragons make everything complicated.

People try to talk to you about them
when you don't want to talk.

How's the old dragon today, hmmm? OK?

Then when you DO want to talk,
they're too busy or they don't want to listen
or they don't understand.
Or THEY want to do all the talking.

You make silly mistakes
because of the dragons.

People don't understand this.
If you explained, they'd think
you were weird.
So you don't.

You don't want to think about dragons but you do, all the time.
How do you spell CAT?
d-r-a-g-o-n
Big, bigger, . . .?
dragon-sized.
Who are you?
A dragon.
2 + 2 =?
4 dragons
2 x 6 =?
12 dragons

ESPECIALLY when you put out the light.
So sometimes I don't.

Now you've got dragons you can't get away from them. They pop up everywhere:

when you wake up, when you clean your teeth,

when you go to school, when you eat lunch,

when you walk home,

when you play games,

when you switch on the television, when you go to bed,

when you put out the light.

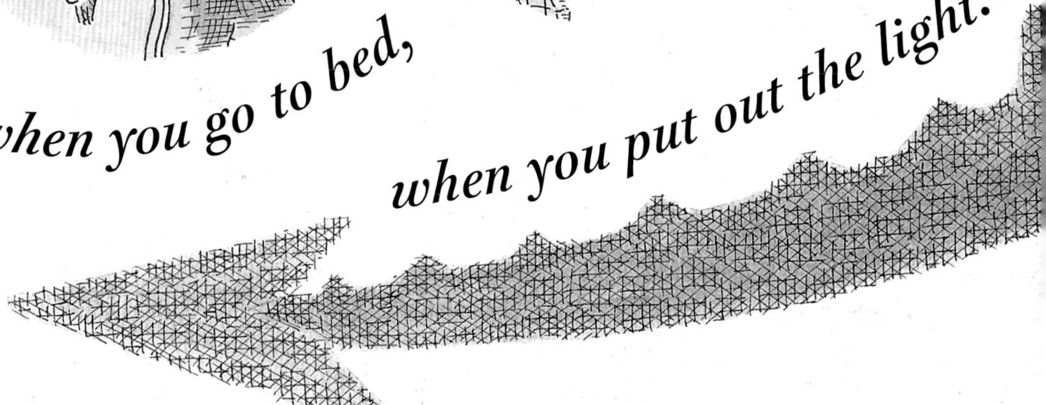

It's a mouse. Who's scared of a mouse?

**Deep down, you KNOW it's a dragon.
You're still scared.**

Then you say:

OK, it's there – but it isn't a dragon.

Some mouse!

Look at its shadow.

That mouse looks just like a dragon.

Pretending a huge, great, ENORMOUS dragon isn't there is exhausting.
So sooner or later you stop.

Dragons are scary.
You try to pretend yours isn't there.

But it IS.

Pretending it isn't there is VERY hard work.

You keep checking to make sure. You have to check in all sorts of places. Sometimes you think it really ISN'T there.

But it IS.

You say to yourself:

*Why me? Why am I the one to get dragons?
Was it something I did? I've been bad sometimes,
but not THAT bad. And mostly I'm good.
I've never been bad enough to deserve THIS.*

**You're right. Nobody deserves dragons.
YOU certainly don't.
You didn't get them by being bad.**

**All these people have
dragons, and they're
FRIGHTFULLY good.**

**You've never had them before.
You're all on your own.**

You’ve got dragons.

You ignore them and you run away from them and you hide from them and you pretend they're not dragons and you shout at them and you don't want to turn out the light and you pay attention to them and you tell them jokes and you can't think of anything else and then suddenly …

Hmm … Something feels different. I wonder what?

Dragons go when you least expect it.
You wake up and they've . . . GONE.

Yours has.
It *really* has.

After all your hard work,
your dragon has gone.

Congratulations! HURRAY! *Well done!*

(And you'll never EVER get dragons so badly again.)

ANCIENT DRAGON WISDOM
On your way through the world, keep your eyes wide open.
Dragons come in all shapes and sizes.
They don't all look the same.
They don't all LOOK like dragons.
They don't all mean us harm.
Honour the dragons that you meet and learn from them.
They are not as powerful as you think.
No dragon is more powerful than YOU.